A FROG PRINCE

written and illustrated by

Alix Berenzy

Henry Holt and Company·New York

To my mother and father

Copyright © 1989 by Alix Berenzy
All rights reserved, including the right to reproduce
this book or portions thereof in any form.
Published by Henry Holt and Company, Inc.,
115 West 18th Street, New York, New York 10011.
Published in Canada by Fitzhenry & Whiteside Limited,
195 Allstate Parkway, Markham, Ontario L3R 4T8.

Library of Congress Cataloging-in-Publication Data
Berenzy, Alix.
The Frog Prince.
Based on the original story: Der Froschkönig.
Summary: Rebuffed by the princess after
retrieving her golden ball, a noble frog sets
out to find a more suitable mate.
[1. Fairy tales]   I. Froschkönig.
II. Title.
PZ8.B84477Fr   1989   [E]   88-29628

ISBN 0-8050-0426-2 (hardcover)
3   5   7   9   10   8   6   4   2
ISBN 0-8050-1848-4 (paperback)
3   5   7   9   10   8   6   4   2

First published in hardcover in 1989 by
Henry Holt and Company, Inc.
First Owlet paperback edition, 1991

Designed by Maryann Leffingwell
Printed in the United States of America

A FROG PRINCE

Once upon a time there lived a Frog who loved a Princess. From the edge of his swamp the Frog would watch the Princess as she played in the Royal Gardens. She never came near the water, but the Frog liked to admire her bright silk dresses and hear her careless laugh. On warm summer evenings he sang love songs to her in a deep froggy voice, but the Princess never seemed to notice.

One day the Frog was sitting in the water, his eye on a fat black fly, when he heard the sound of sobbing. He could hardly believe it was the Princess he saw, crying and lamenting at the water's edge.

Quickly he swam over to her and asked, "What is the matter, Princess? Your tears would move a heart of stone."

The Princess glanced down at him. "My lovely golden ball has fallen into the swamp!" she wailed. Then an idea came into her head. She squeezed even more tears out of her eyes and said, "If you get it for me, I shall let you be my friend. You will eat dinner with me at the castle, and sleep there too!"

The frog was thrilled—though he gladly would have retrieved her toy without a reward. He popped his head under the water, found her ball, and threw it onto the grass beside her.

The Princess was filled with joy when she saw it. She picked up the ball and ran off.

At dinnertime that evening the Frog eagerly knocked on the door of the castle. The Princess opened it, but when she saw the Frog, she shut the door again very quickly.

The King was sitting at the table with all his courtiers. He had seen the Frog, and overheard what had happened in the garden that day. "What you have promised you must honor," he said to his daughter. "Go and open the door for him!"

So the Frog came in and excitedly jumped onto a chair next to the Princess. He had a very good time talking with all of the company. Everyone ate a hearty dinner, except for the Princess, who would eat nothing at all.

After dinner the Frog politely asked where he was to sleep. The Princess began to cry, for she did not want the clammy Frog in her pretty room. But the King became angry and said, "You must not despise anyone who has helped you when you were in need!"

The Princess seized the Frog by the wrist, pulled him up the stairs, and flung him into a corner of her room.

"Sleep *there* if you can, you hideous toad!" she cried. "How could you ever be the companion of a princess!" She thrust a mirror at him and shrieked, "Look at how ugly you are!" She stamped over to her own silken bed, leaving the Frog huddled on the floor.

The Frog looked closely into the mirror, yet he could see nothing wrong. All the same, he felt as if his heart were broken.

That very night he dreamed the Moon was singing to him:

> *Little green Frog alone at night,*
> *Beauty is in the beholder's sight.*
> *Follow the Sun, then follow me,*
> *To lands beyond, across the sea.*
> *In another kingdom you shall find*
> *A true princess, of a different mind.*

The next morning the Frog came down the stairs and met with the King. "I am going out into the World to seek a princess who can see good in me," said the Frog. "I will follow the Sun and the Moon to find her!"

The King liked the Frog and wished to make amends for what his spoiled daughter had done. "Let me help prepare you for your journey," he said.

He ordered his tailors to sew beautiful clothes for the Frog. A prancing white pony was brought from the stables. When the Frog had been royally dressed, the King himself lifted him into the saddle.

The Frog felt very proud and handsome—almost as if he were a prince!

Just then the Princess came down the stairs. She saw the dressed-up Frog and burst into laughter.

The Frog sadly bowed his head. He rode away from the castle into the forest.

Following the Sun by day and the Moon by night, the Frog journeyed on his pony.

On the third day of his travels, he came upon two trolls. They clutched a golden bird cage between them and with their free hands punched and pummeled each other viciously. Within the cage a white dove was dashed against the bars.

The Frog saw that the helpless bird would soon be killed.

"If you let me hold the prize, you will be able to beat each other much better," he called out, pretending to be helpful.

The trolls glared at him with wicked red eyes, each thinking that the prize now included a fresh frog dinner. They gave the cage to him and fell to fighting even harder. Finally, with two tremendous blows, they knocked each other dead.

The Frog breathed a great sigh of relief. He opened the cage and the dove hopped out.

"You are very clever, Frog Prince," he said, bowing.

"Thank you," said the Frog, "but I am not a prince, only a dressed-up frog."

"Be that as it may, I shall repay your kindness," said the dove. Then he flew off.

The Frog continued on his way. After a while he saw a thin line of smoke rising above the treetops. When he came into a clearing, he saw a great black kettle with a fire burning underneath it.

Dancing around it was a green-faced witch. She muttered incantations as she danced and threw moles' teeth and toad warts into the boiling water. All at once she tossed a small, struggling turtle toward the brew. But the Frog, quick as a wink, flicked out his tongue and caught the poor creature on the end of it. The witch shrieked in fury.

The Frog slipped the turtle into his pocket and plunged into the woods astride his pony. The witch scrambled after them, screeching curses and trying her best to cast a spell as she ran. The little horse was so terrified, he galloped like the wind, and they began to outdistance the hag.

But as they ran, the forest grew darker and darker . . . and darker still. The witch had managed to cast a spell upon the trees, making their leaves grow so thickly that they blocked out the light. In complete blackness the pony could only stumble along.

The Frog heard the witch crashing through the bushes and getting closer. He puffed out his throat and cried out to the forest for help. Soon the air was filled with the whirl of wings, and the white dove appeared along with hundreds of birds from all parts of the forest.

Together they pecked away at the leaves, creating a trail of sunbeams in the dark woods. The Frog galloped through, and when the witch tried to follow, the birds flew down and pecked her to bits.

The Frog rode toward the Sun until he came to a great misty ocean and could go no farther. But the little turtle peered out of the Frog's pocket and squeaked with joy, for this was his home.

"You are very brave, Frog Prince," said the turtle, "and I shall repay your kindness."

"Thank you," he replied, "but I am only a frog wearing fancy clothes."

The turtle paddled off into the waves. For a long time the Frog puzzled over how he and the pony might cross. Then he saw the head of the little turtle appear out of the surf. Behind him came hundreds of other turtles. The largest one of all pulled herself up onto the shore. "I shall carry you and your horse to the land across the sea," she said.

With all of the others swimming along beside, the turtle carried them over the water, and the grateful Frog was able to continue on his way.

Days and nights passed as the Frog traveled on his pony. By day the Sun beat down on them. They were covered with dust and scratched by thorns. At night they tripped over rocks and heard the cries of unseen creatures in the woods and in the air. It was a long and weary way, but the Frog was determined to find the princess in his dream.

On the seventh night the Moon suddenly disappeared, and in the darkness horse and rider collided with something hard and rough. The Frog ran his fingers across its bumpy surface. It seemed to go on forever. As he was wondering what it might be, he saw a beetle scurrying along the ground.

"Tell me," began the Frog, "what is this that blocks my way?"

The beetle came to an abrupt stop, cocked his head, and stared up at the Frog. "It is the End of the World, of course. What did you think?" he exclaimed. The beetle scuttled off.

The Frog felt as though a rock had been dropped on his heart. Despairing and exhausted, he lay down on the ground, pulling his crimson cloak around him. The tired pony leaned against the End of the World. Soon they were fast asleep.

The Sun was rising when they awoke. In the early-morning light the Frog saw that the End of the World was not the end of the world at all, but a vast stone wall. And just over the top he could see the towers of a great castle.

"This must be the kingdom of the princess I've been seeking!" he cried excitedly.

He set the horse free in a nearby meadow. Then he crouched down, took a deep breath, and sprang upward. Up and up he went, over the top of the wall, and disappeared!

The Frog landed with a hard bounce in a courtyard. He hopped through an open window into an empty ballroom and made his way down a long, silent hallway. He came to a stone staircase winding around a tower. He hopped up the stairs one by one. At the very top of the tower was a door. The Frog slowly pushed it open.

Within he saw a bed draped in soft velvet. In the bed, fast asleep, was the most beautiful princess the Frog could ever have imagined.

She was so lovely, the Frog hardly dared to approach. But as he gazed at her, he could not resist leaning down to kiss her.

The Princess slowly opened her golden eyes and sat up. "Is it morning already?" she asked. Then she saw the Frog standing there. "Where have you come from, Frog Prince?" she said in wonder.

The Frog told her of his adventures and how he had finally come to find her. "But I am not a prince," he said, "only a common frog."

The Princess looked upon him with shining eyes. "Your deeds have been noble," she said. "Is not what we do proof of what we are? With all of my heart, I believe you *are* a real prince." Then she added shyly, "Certainly you are as handsome as one."

The Frog blushed a deep green. When he had recovered, he said, "I shall love and honor you all the days of my life."

"Then let us be married," said the Princess, for she too had fallen in love.

They hopped down the stairs together. All the servants, who had been asleep in their rooms, came out and rejoiced when they saw the lovely couple. Salamanders rang silver bells, and the old turtle cook prepared a fabulous wedding feast. A great lumpy toad married them and declared them King and Queen as well as husband and wife, and all the company cheered.

Then there was a wild dance to the tune of crickets chirping and little tree frogs singing. Everyone danced for three days and three nights.

The Frog soon forgot the King's spoiled daughter and his unhappy time with her. His love for the Frog Queen grew, and they reigned together in peace.

The Frog King and Queen lived very happily in their castle in that deep wood. And I would venture to say they are living there still.